Humphrey's

Birthday

For Ralph
Love Mum
x

PUFFIN BOOKS

Published by the Penguin Group
Penguin Books Ltd, 80 Strand, London WC2R ORL, England
Penguin Putnam Inc., 375 Hudson Street, New York, New York 10014, USA
Penguin Books Australia Ltd, 250 Camberwell Road, Camberwell, Victoria 3124, Australia
Penguin Books Canada Ltd, 10 Alcorn Avenue, Toronto, Ontario, Canada M4V 3B2
Penguin Books India (P) Ltd, 11 Community Centre, Panchsheel Park, New Delhi – 110 017, India
Penguin Books (NZ) Ltd, Cnr Rosedale and Airborne Roads, Albany, Auckland, New Zealand
Penguin Books (South Africa) (Pty) Ltd, 24 Sturdee Avenue, Rosebank 2196, South Africa

Penguin Books Ltd, Registered Offices: 80 Strand, London WC2R ORL, England

First published 2003
3 5 7 9 10 8 6 4 2

Copyright © Sally Hunter, 2003

Made and printed in Singapore by Tien Wah Press (Pte) Ltd

British Library Cataloguing in Publication Data
A CIP catalogue record for this book is available from the British Library

ISBN 0-670-91065-1

To find out more about Humphrey's world, visit the web site at:
www.humphreys-corner.com

This edition produced for The Book People Ltd,
Hall Wood Avenue, Haydock, St Helens WA11 9UL

Humphrey's

Birthday

Sally Hunter

TED SMART

It was a very special day.
It was Humphrey's birthday!

Humphrey had some lovely presents.

Baby Jack kept trying
to help open them!

Lottie made a fairy card,
with lots of glitter on,
and a painted stone.

Baby Jack gave a rainbow pencil with a
rubber on the end, but it was a bit
soppy because he had sucked it.

And Daddy bought Humphrey a painted
boat with a whale
and a fish
and a crocodile inside it.

But Humphrey's most
favourite present
was a real, proper
superhero suit.

WOW!

It had bright colours
and a shiny,
floaty cloak.

Humphrey could
do really big jumps now...

...and fly very high.

Humphrey said he thought
it must be a very magic cloak.

Mummy said, "Let's go and see if anyone
needs rescuing. Downstairs."

All morning Humphrey was a very big help. He flew to the ceiling for Daddy...

... and fetched important things Mummy needed – super quick!

Mummy said it was nearly time for Humphrey's party! Humphrey was very excited!

He kept jumping up and looking out of the window to see if anyone was coming...

...and jumping back down again!

But when everyone arrived, Humphrey stopped
jumping and stayed near Mummy. He was a bit shy.

There was George, Humphrey's little friend
(who lived next door), and his mummy and
baby Daisy.

Lottie's best, best
friend Jessie...

...and Granny, Grandad and cousin Emma...

...who loved Humphrey very much!

Humphrey had some more lovely presents:

 a little book with some colour pencils inside from George,

a knitted jumper from Granny and Grandad,

 a ladybird that Emma had made all by herself

and a very bouncy ball from Jessie.

Mummy said the fairies knew it was
Humphrey's birthday too and maybe they had
left some surprises in the garden.

Then they played pass the parcel and Emma won.
She was very pleased!

Grandad gave all the children
some bubbly pots.
Everybody was having a lovely time.

Daddy got the paddling pool out of the shed.
He put lots of bubble mixture in and filled it up
with warm water.

Lottie got very excited and jumped and ran
around even more, shouting,
"Yippee!"

But Humphrey wasn't too sure.
Mop couldn't swim and he really didn't
want to take his special outfit off.

But then, because Jessie was there ...

Lottie was a little bit silly.

S P L O S H ! !

Humphrey was wet

ALL OVER !

Humphrey was very, very upset...

...even though it was his special day
and he was such a big boy.

Daddy had a quiet chat
with Lottie...

...and Mummy said not to worry because
Humphrey was magic so he would soon dry...

...and that superheroes did
get wet sometimes.

Lottie said she was sorry
like she properly meant it.

Then Mummy called, "Tea time!"

What a lovely birthday tea!

There were Humphrey's
favourite sandwiches,

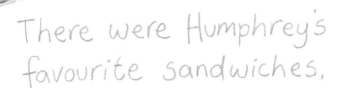

 animal biscuits,

juicy grapes,

Granny's cherry cakes,

popcorn,

 cheese on sticks,

apple juice with bubbles in

and Mummy's very special...

...BIRTHDAY CAKE!

Happy birthday,

dear Humphrey!